JE

D1530978

4-99

ACA4319-7

CL

Copyright © 1985 by Nord-Süd Verlag AG, Gossau Zürich, Switzerland
First published in Switzerland under the title *Jonathan, die freche Maus*
English language edition copyright © 1985 by North-South Books.

First published in the Great Britain, Canada,
Australia, and New Zealand in 1985 by North-South Books,
an imprint of Nord-Süd Verlag AG, Gossau Zürich, Switzerland. First
published in the United States in 1986 by North-South Books.
First paperback edition published in 1997.

Distributed in the United States by North-South Books Inc., New York.

Library of Congress Cataloging-in-Publication Data
Ostheeren, Ingrid
Jonathan Mouse
Translation of: Jonathan die freche Maus.
Summary: A group of farmyard animals comes to a mouse's aid when
a spell dooms him to turn the same color as everything he eats.
[1. Mice—Fiction. 2. Domestic animals—Fiction. 3. Color-Fiction]
I. Mathieu, Agnes, Ill. II Title.
PZ7.0847Jo 1986 [Fic} 85-10501

A CIP catalogue record for this book is available from The British Library.

ISBN 1-55858-780-2 (paperback)
1 3 5 7 9 PB 10 8 6 4 2
Printed in Belgium

For more information about our books, and the authors and artists
who create them, visit our web site: http://www.northsouth.com

Jonathan
MOUSE

Ingrid Ostheeren

Illustrated by
Agnès Mathieu

Translated by
Rosemary Lanning

North-South Books
New York   London

There was once a little mouse who tried to steal some bacon from a bad fairy. Well, she wasn't really a bad fairy – just an old lady who knew a bit of magic. She caught the little mouse, but then let it go, saying, "Silly little mouse. To teach you a lesson, I'll make you the color of everything you eat from now on!"

The mouse, whose name was Jonathan by the way, wasn't the least bit worried by her threat. He stuck out his tongue at her and ran away.

On his way home he came to a farm, and because he was hungry the little mouse decided to stop and look for something to eat. He found a carrot, and was nibbling away at it happily when Toby, the farm dog, came up behind him and growled: "What kind of creature are you?"

"I'm a mouse, silly!" said Jonathan, with as much dignity as possible.

Toby shook his head. "Mice are gray," he said.

"But I am gray," snapped Jonathan. "Mousey gray, you could say."

"You're mouse-shaped," admitted Toby after a few moments' thought, "but you're not mouse-colored."

Jonathan took a deep breath and was just about to set the dog straight when he looked down at himself. It was true! He wasn't gray. He was the color of …"Carrots!"he whispered, horrified.

Then he remembered the old woman and he told Toby what she had said.

"You mean you're going to turn the same color as everything you eat?" said Toby, thoughtfully.

"I'm afraid so," he replied.

They decided to put this to the test. Toby fetched a bit of tomato, a bit of Swiss cheese, a cabbage leaf, a piece of chocolate and a plum. Jonathan pushed the plum aside at once. He couldn't stand purple!

First Jonathan took a hefty bite from the tomato and then he looked at himself. His fur turned red. Horrified, he threw the rest of the tomato away. "Red is a stupid color for a mouse," he muttered. "A cat would have to be blind not to see me. The very thought takes my appetite away."

All the same, he tackled the Swiss cheese and instantly turned a cheesy yellow. Reluctantly, he began to gnaw at the cabbage leaf. A pale shimmer of green spread over his fur.

Toby thought this was great! The green then changed to brown as Jonathan chomped a mouthful of chocolate, his cheeks bulging.

"Brown isn't bad," said Toby in an encouraging way, shooing off a couple of nosy hens who had come clucking along.

"You like it because your own coat is brown," said Jonathan. "But I'm supposed to be *gray* – a beautiful mousey gray." Moodily he pulled a couple of forget-me-nots out of the flower-bed and gulped them down. He didn't care what color he became.

Jonathan and Toby lay down beside each other in silence. Suddenly Jonathan sobbed, and a tear ran down his forget-me-not blue face. "I wish . . . I wish I was gray again," he whispered sadly.

"This won't do!" Toby said as he stood up. "Come on, let's go and ask the other animals for advice." Jonathan nodded gratefully.

First they asked the cows, grazing under the apple trees, and the two goats in front of the farmhouse.

Next they trotted along to the pigsty, where their arrival set off a wild grunting, squealing, pushing and shoving. All the pigs wanted to see the forget-me-not blue mouse.

Then they asked the two farm horses in their stable, the four rabbits in their hutches and the cock in the yard. But none of the animals had any advice to give.

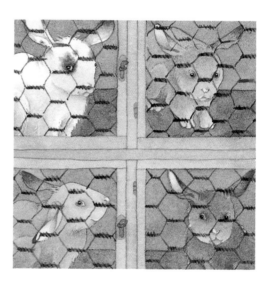

"That just leaves the cat," said Toby.

"Are you crazy?" said Jonathan. "He'll eat me!"

"Me? Eat *you*?" growled the cat from right above him. "As if I would!"

Toby told Jonathan's story. The cat yawned and stretched. "Let me know when he's gray again," she murmured lazily, and closed her eyes.

Sadly, the friends flopped down next to the flower-bed again. Suddenly Toby raised his head. "I've got an idea!" he cried. "You should eat something gray — I know just the thing!" Toby ran off, and returned as fast as his legs would carry him.

"What have you found?" asked Jonathan.

"A bit of the farmer's best trousers. The nicest gray I could find."

"Oh no!" groaned Jonathan. "Must I?"

"Eat it!" commanded Toby.

Bravely, Jonathan began to chew and his coat turned grayer and grayer, until finally a mouse-gray mouse stood in front of Toby.

"Well, how do I look?" asked Jonathan cheerfully.

"Wonderful! Really mousey!" said Toby. Now they were both happy — but not for long!

"I've just thought of something awful," sobbed Jonathan. "I'll have to eat farmers' trousers for the rest of my life. And they taste horrible!" He shuddered.

Once again they both lay there, feeling miserable. Jonathan nibbled absent-mindedly at the rest of the tomato.

AND HE DIDN'T TURN RED! NOT AT ALL! NOT ONE TINY BIT!

"You didn't turn red," stammered Toby.

"Well, why should I?" replied Jonathan sleepily. "I feel fine."

"But you ate a tomato."

"A tomato!" Jonathan sat up, shocked, and peered at his paws. Right forepaw – all right. Left forepaw – all right, mouse-gray, as it should be.

"Hey, Jonathan, I think that stupid magic has worn off," whispered Toby.

"Great!" cried Jonathan, and jumped up and down. But then the cat came slinking across the yard.

"Toby! Here comes the cat! 'Bye, and thanks!"
Jonathan scampered out of the gate and ran for his life.
Toby looked sternly at the cat.
"Were you really going to eat him?"
The cat looked ashamed — but not very.
"He was such a delicious gray," she murmured.
Then she strolled away.